**QUICKREADS**

# READ MY LIPS

JANICE GREENE

# QUICKREADS

### SERIES 1
Black Widow Beauty
Danger on Ice
Empty Eyes
The Experiment
The Kula'i Street Knights
The Mystery Quilt
No Way to Run
The Ritual
The 75-Cent Son
The Very Bad Dream

### SERIES 2
The Accuser
Ben Cody's Treasure
Blackout
The Eye of the Hurricane
The House on the Hill
Look to the Light
Ring of Fear
The Tiger Lily Code
Tug-of-War
The White Room

### SERIES 3
The Bad Luck Play
Breaking Point
Death Grip
Fat Boy
No Exit
No Place Like Home
The Plot
Something Dreadful Down Below
Sounds of Terror
The Woman Who Loved a Ghost

### SERIES 4
The Barge Ghost
Beasts
Blood and Basketball
Bus 99
The Dark Lady
Dimes to Dollars
**Read My Lips**
Ruby's Terrible Secret
Student Bodies
Tough Girl

www.sdlback.com

**Copyright ©2010, 2005 by Saddleback Educational Publishing**
All rights reserved. No part of this book may be reproduced or transmitted in any form or by any means, electronic or mechanical, including photocopying, recording, or by any information storage and retrieval system, without the written permission of the publisher.

ISBN-13: 978-1-61651-216-3
ISBN-10: 1-61651-216-4
eBook: 978-1-60291-938-9

Printed in Guangzhou, China
0310/03-20-10

15 14 13 12 11   1 2 3 4 5

■ ■ ■

Lupe Herrera stood in front of Schmidt's desk, trying to control her temper. "I'm not the enemy," she said.

Lieutenant Schmidt crossed his thick arms over his chest. "I never said I had a problem with you, Lupe."

"True," she said. "You've never said much of anything. But I haven't been given the cooperation I need from you and the rest of the squad."

"Okay, okay," Schmidt said, turning toward his computer. "I'll see that you get all the cooperation you need."

"One more thing, sir," she added.

Schmidt sighed and looked back at her reluctantly.

"I'd really appreciate it," she went on, "if you'd turn around and look at me when you're speaking to me."

"Oh, yeah. Right," he said. "Sorry. I keep forgetting about—"

"—my being deaf," Lupe finished for him. "That's one reason," she said stiffly. "But mainly, I'd appreciate being treated with a little more respect."

"*Fine!*" Schmidt said impatiently.

"Thank you very much," Lupe said as she walked out of Schmidt's office, silently fuming. Detective Harris glanced up from his desk and scowled at her.

"You're looking very well today, Detective," Lupe said brightly. He grunted in reply.

Detective Diego Molina also looked up at her. Then he nodded and smiled sympathetically. He was the only male in the squad who'd treated Lupe as a fellow professional.

Lupe returned to her desk, which was just outside Schmidt's office.

She began to read a file, when a young man wearing a big smile walked in the squadroom door.

"Hey, guys!" he called out. He held a box of cigars.

"Hey!" Detective Harris greeted him in return. "It's the new dad!"

Everyone crowded around the young man, slapping him on the back. He looked exhausted and happy.

Lieutenant Schmidt called out, "How's the baby, Detective? Your little guy ready for officer's training yet?"

All the men laughed. Glancing over at Lupe, the young detective said, "Who's sitting at my desk?"

Lupe could only guess that he had lowered his voice. What he didn't know was that she could read his lips—and everyone else's.

Schmidt's look was derisive. "Oh, she's been sent here from the mayor's office," he said. "She's part of that stupid 'job efficiency' task force."

"Huh? What's that?" the young detective asked nervously.

"They think they can pop in here, snoop

through our timesheets, and tell us how to work more efficiently," Schmidt said with a sneer. "But I'm sure she'll just shuffle some paper, write up a report on us for some idiot at the mayor's office, and be gone in a week." He laughed and then snarled, "Like we don't know how to do the job right in the first place!"

The men all nodded in agreement.

The young detective held out the box of cigars. "Light up, guys," he said.

Schmidt turned and looked directly at Lupe. "I'm *shocked*, Detective! You know that smoking's not allowed in government buildings. We light up in here and she might just tell on us!" He looked back at the men. "At least that would be one thing the super snoop could report to the mayor!" He laughed loudly.

Then Schmidt took the box and held it out to Lupe. "Care for a cigar?" he offered. His tone was taunting. Behind him, the men had suddenly gone silent. Several were smirking.

Lupe looked at him coolly. "No, thank you,"

she said. "I don't smoke. But please don't let me stop *you*."

Then Schmidt deliberately lit his cigar, inhaled deeply, and blew out a plume of smoke in Lupe's direction. One by one, the other men followed suit. The air in the Southern Police Station quickly became a gray haze.

Lupe had tried cigarettes when she was younger, and hated them. Now, the thick cigar smoke in the room was actually making her feel sick.

Schmidt went back into his office, plopped down in his chair, and opened a large lunch bag. He was a big man with a big appetite. Unwrapping a huge sandwich, he wrapped his thick fingers around it and took a bite.

The heavy smells of cheese, pickles, and salami drifted through Schmidt's door. Lupe felt nauseated. *Don't look,* she told herself. She didn't want to see any food right now.

She looked. Schmidt was chewing a huge mouthful. A ragged piece of lettuce hung from his lips. Watery mustard dripped down his wrist.

Lupe got up, feeling a little faint. She started walking toward the restroom. Then she ran. The men's laughter followed her.

■ ■ ■

The next morning, Lupe woke up with a start. Her alarm clock hadn't gone off. The alarm, which woke her up by vibrating, wasn't under her pillow. She looked around and finally found it on the floor. When she looked at the time, she groaned. She'd be late!

Lupe hurried into the squadroom hoping Schmidt wouldn't notice her—and make some cutting remark. But Schmidt was across the room, talking to several officers. She saw him say, "Toya's back in San Francisco." She moved to a spot where she could watch him better.

"He's got a girlfriend who lives at 901 Folsom, fifth floor," Schmidt went on. "What I'd like to do is put a bug in there. But getting in will be tricky. Toya's probably got lookouts on duty around the clock."

"I know that block," Lupe blurted out. "Maybe I could read his lips from the building across the street. Sooner or later he'd probably say something you'd be able to use on him."

Schmidt gave her a blank look. The other men stared, surprised. Diego said, "That could work! We wouldn't need a bug if she could read his lips."

Lieutenant Schmidt was silent. Then he nodded slowly. "It's worth a try, I guess," he said. "If I can get permission from the mayor's office, you can take Lupe over there, Diego, and see if this idea will work."

Lupe's heart hammered in her chest. What had she gotten herself into?

■ ■ ■

Two hours later, Lupe and Diego were headed toward Folsom Street. She watched him as he drove. His, hands, broad and strong looking, rested lightly on the wheel.

"Who's this guy, Toya?" she asked.

"He's a thief," Diego said. "A really bold one. He'll rob a place in broad daylight. Specializes in big-ticket items. He knows what's valuable and who'll buy it."

"A real bad guy, huh? Has he ever done time?" asked Lupe.

"Not a single day," Diego said. "Last year we caught two of his people. They wouldn't say a thing about him. They're really loyal—or scared." He gave her a warm smile and said, "Hey, I'm real sorry about that cigar deal yesterday. You looked kind of green. Are you okay now?"

"Yeah, I'm okay," Lupe said. "But I must admit that Schmidt drives me crazy sometimes."

Diego laughed. "He really resents anyone from the mayor's office telling him what to do."

"More like he doesn't want *anyone* telling him what to do," said Lupe.

Diego laughed again. "You've got that right," he said. "Plus, you're a woman—and he's an old-school guy."

Maybe it was the warmth of his eyes that made Lupe give in to a sudden impulse. "Are you seeing anyone?" she blurted out.

"Uh—" he stuttered. The back of his neck had turned red.

"No! Never mind!" she broke in. "I didn't mean to say that. Sometimes I'm so stupid," she finished in a murmur. She wished she could just jump out of the car and run.

Nothing else was said until they reached 901 Folsom Street. It was a five-story apartment building. Its blue paint had faded almost to white. Lupe glanced up and saw that most people on the upper floors left their curtains open. She hoped Toya's girlfriend was one of them.

The building on the other side of the street was six stories tall. Good! A room in front would make a great lookout spot.

"Looks like a go," said Diego. "Let's head back." Now his manner seemed distant, formal. Lupe's foolish outburst hung between them like a brick wall.

■ ■ ■

Later that day, Lupe returned to the Folsom Street building. She was partnered with Detective Harris. Lupe was perched on a chair by the window. Beside her, Detective Harris sat as still as a stone. His sharp-angled face and thick red hair made her think of a fox.

Across the street, 901 Folsom was dotted with lighted windows. Luckily, the curtains were open in Toya's girlfriend's apartment.

There was a man inside sitting on a couch. The light from a TV flickered from across the room. Lupe peered through the high-powered telescope. She wondered if he was Toya.

Harris finally spoke up. "The guy doesn't even get up for commercials."

Lupe nodded. They'd been watching for two hours now, and the man hadn't moved. About 30 years old, he had dark, wavy hair, a strong chin, and confident eyes.

Suddenly a movement inside the room caught Lupe's eye. Her fingers shook with excitement as Detective Harris whipped out a notebook and pen from his jacket.

Two men walked into the room and stood in front of the couch. One, a thin man with a mustache, had on a gray leather jacket. The other, tall and bulky, wore a dark blue sweater.

Lupe spoke rapidly. "Blue sweater says he can get the truck by the end of the week," she reported.

Harris wrote down what Lupe said.

Still looking at the TV, the man on the couch said, "I need it tomorrow." The authority in his voice suggested he was the boss—Toya.

The man in the blue sweater ran a nervous hand through his hair. "He's not sure he can do that—" he said.

Then he bent toward Toya, as if hoping for an answer. But Toya didn't say a word—or even move.

Blue sweater said, "Okay, boss, we'll just tell him—"

Then a door behind them opened. A

young blonde woman walked in the room. She held out a cell phone to Toya.

Toya gave the others a quick look of dismissal, and they left the room.

Then he put the phone to his ear, listened, and said, "Good." After a long silence, he said, "Right. Nine o'clock."

Lupe repeated Toya's words as Harris bent over his notebook.

Then Toya left the room.

"Darn!" Lupe groaned. Harris looked up and swore.

"Maybe he'll come back," Lupe said faintly.

Harris snorted.

They waited another hour, then another. Finally, the woman came back in the room and turned off the light. Lupe and Harris were done for the day.

■ ■ ■

The next day at the station, Lieutenant Schmidt called Lupe to his office. Harris was already there. His sharp, fox-like face looked intense.

"There's been a robbery in Pacific Heights," Schmidt said. "Three blocks from the last one. Guys from the Northern Station have already been there. But I want you two to see if the robber could've been Toya. The family was home when it happened."

He turned to Lupe. "You any good with kids?"

"Sure," Lupe said eagerly.

"That's good," Schmidt grumbled, "because Harris scares 'em."

She and Harris got up to leave. "Lieutenant? What time did the robbery take place?" Lupe asked.

"Uh—it was nine o'clock," Schmidt replied. "Yeah," he added, "I saw it in Harris' report. The guy on the phone said, 'nine o'clock.' Maybe it means something. Maybe it doesn't."

■ ■ ■

About 40 minutes later, Lupe and Harris were at the robbery scene in Pacific Heights. Lupe sat on a chair made of dark, carved wood. The arms were so smooth, they felt silky. The deep, rich colors in the carpet were woven in intricate designs. Lupe had lived in San Francisco all her life, but she'd never been inside a house in this posh neighborhood before. She felt like a visitor in a foreign country.

Across from her and Harris sat Gordon and Emily deWildt. Their son, Trevor, sat between them. He was a sturdy-looking boy, about five years old. On his arm was a slightly dirty cast, nearly covered with signatures.

"They took the big-screen TV, a lot of clothes, the computers—" Gordon was saying.

"They took my PlayStation, too. It was new," Trevor piped up.

"Yes, sweetheart," Emily said. She turned to Harris. "The first officers who came know all this. Do we really have to go through it again?"

"Yes, ma'am, we do," Harris said impatiently. "Did one of the thieves seem to be the man in charge?"

"Yes," said Gordon. "He had dark hair. That's all I can remember."

Harris stood up. "How tall was he? About my height?"

"Taller," Emily suggested.

"No, about three inches shorter," Gordon corrected her.

Harris' mouth tightened. "Weight?" he asked.

"I guess it seemed about right for his height," Gordon said.

Harris started tapping his foot on the carpet impatiently. "Anything unusual about his looks?"

"No," Gordon said, his voice now sounding ragged with exhaustion.

"He looked *heartless*," Emily added before covering her mouth as she fought back tears.

Gordon stood up. "That's enough," he said harshly. "In case you've forgotten, we're the victims—not the criminals."

Reluctantly, Harris stood up.

"Sorry!" Lupe said. "I know you folks have been through a lot. We're really grateful for what you've told us." She turned to Trevor. "Could I sign your cast before we leave?"

she asked.

"Sure!" Trevor said excitedly.

Lupe took a pen from her pocket.

Trevor held up his cast, and Lupe wrote her name on a bare spot.

"I remember something," the boy said. "He had a snake."

"Who had a snake?" Lupe asked.

"The guy who was the boss," Trevor said. He pointed to his wrist. "It was right here."

"You saw a drawing of a snake? A tattoo?" Lupe asked.

"Yeah," Trevor said confidently.

Then Emily interrupted. "Trevor! Those men were wearing gloves."

"Yeah," Trevor said, "but they were the see-through kind."

"You mean like the thin rubber ones that doctors wear?" Lupe asked.

Trevor thought for a moment. "Yes," he said. "And sometimes nurses, too."

"Good work, Trevor," Lupe said with a smile. "You're a real detective."

Trevor beamed.

As they drove off, Lupe was hoping Harris would compliment her for her good work, but he didn't say a word.

■ ■ ■

The next morning, Schmidt came in early. "Listen up, kids," he said. "Here's 'Plan B' on Toya. We're sending Diego in to plant a bug."

Lupe glanced over at Diego, but he quickly looked away.

Schmidt went on. "Tomorrow night, Diego will go in to the girlfriend's apartment. Harris, you and I will be watching from across the street. Lupe, you can come, too—if you want."

■ ■ ■

The night was clear and sharply cold. Harris kept rubbing his hands together. Schmidt pulled his scarf up over his ears and wolfed down a candy bar. Lupe was glad she couldn't hear him. She went back to the telescope. She'd been watching for almost an hour.

At ten minutes after eight, Toya rose from his spot on the couch. He turned to someone outside the room and said, "Chicken again, Raymond?" Then he got up and left the room.

"Chicken again, Raymond?" Lupe murmured.

"Are you *sure* that's what he said?" Harris asked Lupe.

"It looks like he's headed out," Schmidt said as he took a cell phone from his pocket.

A few minutes later, Toya and the woman came out of the building. A car pulled up, and they both got inside.

Harris flipped open his phone and said, "Diego? *Go!*"

Lupe saw Diego come from the side street and walk into the building. Her breath came short and fast.

Lupe, Schmidt, and Harris waited. Ten minutes. Twenty minutes.

"He should've been out by now," Harris muttered to Schmidt.

Schmidt stirred restlessly.

"Look!" Lupe whispered.

Toya's car turned onto the street and pulled up in front of the building. Schmidt swore.

■ ■ ■

Toya and another man got out of the car and entered the building.

A minute later, Toya was in the apartment. Schmidt said, "Harris! Go downstairs! Get to the car!" Harris hurried away. Then Schmidt turned to Lupe. "Watch him!" he snapped. But Lupe was already at the telescope.

The man from the car stood right in front of Toya. Lupe couldn't see their mouths. "Move! *Move!*" she whispered.

Another man walked into the room. Lupe gasped. There was a dark streak of blood on his shirt!

"I put him in the bathtub," the man reported to Toya. "Didn't want his blood messing up your girl's apartment!" He chuckled coldheartedly as he brushed at the stain on his shirt.

Lupe couldn't tell if Toya answered. "They've put Diego in the bathtub," she whispered to Schmidt, "so—so his blood doesn't mess up the apartment," she continued in a shaky voice.

All three men left the room. Then Toya's girlfriend came in and turned off the light.

Lupe saw Schmidt reach for his phone. She figured it must have rung. "What?" Schmidt demanded. "Yeah, he's definitely hurt. Don't know how bad, though—or even if he's still alive. Hold on. They're coming out now."

Lupe turned the telescope toward the door. She was relieved to see *four* men exit the building. "Lieutenant, look!" Lupe cried out. "Diego's with them. He's okay."

Diego had a cap pulled low over his forehead. Toya and another man were on either side of him. They walked toward the car. As they passed under the street light, Diego lifted his head. He mouthed the words: *"the morgue. Fifth Street."* Then Toya pushed him into the car.

"Diego said, 'The morgue. Fifth Street,'" Lupe reported.

Schmidt scowled. "You got it wrong, Lupe!" he snapped. "There's no morgue on Fifth Street."

He put the phone to his ear. "Harris! Did you see Diego? Lupe says he said, 'The morgue. Fifth Street.' But there's no morgue—. Oh, yeah? You *sure*? Okay. We're there."

"What's happening?" Lupe asked.

Harris snapped the phone shut. "Come on!" he barked.

Schmidt hurried down the stairs and out onto the street. Lupe followed. Harris was in the car and the motor was running. Schmidt got in beside him and immediately started talking. Lupe sat in back. Both men were facing forward.

"Please turn to the side so I can see what you're saying!" Lupe said. "Is there a morgue?"

"I hear that's what they're calling the

old Bascomb building," Schmidt said. "It's been empty for a year, while they retrofit the place," he continued with a frown. "I'm calling for backup."

■ ■ ■

In a few minutes, they pulled up close to the Bascomb building. It was an old, three-story structure, almost half a block wide.

They hurried along the side of the building. In the rear was a small parking lot and a loading dock, about six feet high. A wide iron door to the building's basement was pulled open. Two men pushed dollies across a ramp from the dock to a waiting truck. The dollies were loaded with boxes. Standing just inside the truck, a bald man watched them work.

"You two see anyone familiar?" Schmidt asked.

Lupe shook her head.

"Nope," Harris said, giving Lupe a sour look. "Maybe we're in the wrong place," he added.

"Well, let's just have a look," Schmidt said.

"Lupe, you come too—but stay close to us. Got that?"

Lupe nodded.

They walked up to the loading dock. Schmidt said, "Good evening, gentlemen. I'm Lieutenant Schmidt, San Francisco Police. Can you tell us what's going on here this evening?"

The men stopped their work and stared. Then the bald man said, "We're removing the office furniture. The building's going to be retrofitted. We've got papers, if that's what you people are worried about."

Schmidt waved him off. "I'm sure your papers are in good order," he said. "We just want to look in a few of your boxes."

"Be my guest," the man offered.

Schmidt and Harris climbed onto the loading dock. Big as Schmidt was, he moved as lightly as a cat. He jerked his head toward a large box. "Let's see what's in this one," he said.

A man in a gray leather jacket gave him a bored look and opened the box. He pushed away styrofoam peanuts. Underneath was a computer monitor.

"How about one more?" Schmidt asked, pointing to an oblong box.

The box was opened. Inside was a computer keyboard. Its characters were worn with use.

"Just as I told you, it's all office equipment," the bald man said.

"Right," Schmidt agreed, stepping back. "Well, thank you for your time, gentlemen."

The man in the gray leather jacket smiled just a little.

As she was about to turn away, Lupe noticed a drop of something wet on the man's shoe. It was shiny—and red.

"Let's go," Schmidt said to Harris and Lupe. When they turned to leave, Lupe whispered, "The man in the gray leather jacket—I think I saw a drop of blood on his shoe."

Schmidt stared at her. Then, in a low, growly voice, he said, "Get back to the car. And stay down."

■ ■ ■

Lupe hurried across the parking lot. As she turned the corner, she glanced back. Schmidt and Harris were standing in front of the men on the ramp. She couldn't see their faces, so she got in the car.

The minutes ticked by. Lupe shivered. She was imagining Diego lying somewhere, bleeding. Waiting was pure torture.

Then a car pulled up several spaces away. Four detectives from the station hustled out and started to head toward the parking lot.

Lupe's mind raced. What if there was shooting? She wished desperately that she could hear!

Just then a man turned the corner at a run. He had dark, wavy hair and a strong chin. *Toya!* Lupe gulped. She slid down low, behind the headrest. Then Harris turned the corner.

As Toya approached, she unlocked the door and grasped the handle. Toya was four feet away. Two feet away. *Get it right!*

she thought to herself.

*Now!* She whispered.

Lupe shoved open the door just as Toya came by. The bottom corner of the door hit his heel. He tumbled to the sidewalk. As he fell, Lupe caught a glimpse of the tattoo on his wrist. It was a cobra, poised to strike!

In an instant, Harris was on him. With one knee on Toya's back, Harris yanked the man's arms behind his back. Then he snapped on handcuffs.

Finally, Harris looked up at Lupe. His eyebrows were raised in amazement. Then he jerked Toya to his feet and walked him back to the parking lot.

For awhile Lupe couldn't tell what was happening. Finally, Schmidt returned to the car alone.

"Is Diego—" Lupe asked.

"Yeah, he's okay," Schmidt said. "They roughed him up pretty bad, but thanks to you, we got here before they could finish the job. And it looks like we've rounded up the whole herd. Those other guys we saw in the apartment on Folsom were in the basement. Toya went out the side door, but Harris got him." He grinned at her. "I heard Harris had a little help."

Lupe smiled. She was amazed that Harris had given her credit.

■ ■ ■

The next day, Lupe was bent over her desk. She had piles of work now that Schmidt had given her the information she needed. Suddenly, a hand slapped down in front of her. She jumped. It was Harris. His sharp fox face twitched. Lupe laughed. She knew that, for Harris, it was a smile.

Then Schmidt stopped by her desk with a huge box of jelly donuts. He held the open box out to her and said, "Have one, Lupe. A good detective's day isn't complete if it doesn't start out with a donut."

Then she noticed an e-mail from Diego. "To answer your question," he wrote, "I'm not seeing anyone. Want to go out for dinner tonight?"

Lupe looked over at Diego. There was a hopeful look on his badly bruised face. She mouthed the words, *It's a date!* From the smile that lit up Diego's face, it was clear that this time, *he* had been the successful lip reader. Lupe closed her eyes and smiled. For now, life couldn't be sweeter.

# After-Reading Wrap-Up

1. At the beginning of the story, Lupe met with a lot of hostility in the squadroom. For what two main reasons did the detectives resent her presence? (Hint: Her physical disability is *not* one of them.)

2. Think about how the author depicted Lt. Schmidt. Do you think he was intended to be likeable or unlikeable? Give two details of his speech or behavior to support your opinion.

3. What details do you remember about the characters' personalities? Write two adjectives that could be used to describe each of these characters: *Lupe, Diego, Harris.*

4. Diego tells Lupe that Toya specializes in stealing "big-ticket items." What did he mean by that? List four examples of

- Continued -

"big-ticket items."

5. What bold action did Lupe take that finally won the approval of Schmidt, Harris, and the other detectives?

6. What do you think would have happened next if the story had gone on? Would Lupe have continued on as a special assistant to the police department? Or would she have returned to work in the mayor's office? Explain your opinion.